W9-CCP-027

SARB
ANt

Ali Baba
&
the Forty Thieves

Once upon a time, a poor woodcutter named Ali Baba lived in a town in Persia with his wife and son. Each day, Ali Baba took his donkey to a nearby forest and cut wood to sell in town.

2

As he worked in the forest one day, Ali Baba heard the thundering sound of horses' hooves coming toward him. Worried that the riders were robbers, he led his donkey up a tall pile of rocks so they wouldn't be seen. From his hiding spot, Ali Baba counted forty men. By the fine clothes they wore and the swords they carried, he was certain they were thieves.

The riders tied up their horses by a pile of boulders. One man stepped forward, wearing such fine clothes that Ali Baba was sure he was the captain of the thieves.

"Open, sesame!" he shouted.

With that, a large rock rolled aside, revealing a hidden cave. The men stepped inside, and the rock rolled back into place, sealing the secret opening behind them.

Ali Baba was astonished! He was very curious about the cave, but decided to stay hidden until it was safe. After some time, the thieves came out carrying bags that looked quite heavy, and loaded them onto their horses. After they rode away, Ali Baba climbed down from his perch.

Ali Baba walked over to the rocks and shouted, "Open, sesame!" just as the captain had done.

The rock door rolled aside, revealing a cave full of treasure. There were heaps of glittering coins and jewelry, piles of luxurious silks and rugs, and many beautiful candelabras and statues. It was dazzling!

Ali Baba stepped inside, and the door closed behind him. Worried that the robbers would return, he quickly gathered some gold coins, taking as much as his donkey could carry. When he was ready to go, he said, "Open, sesame," and the door opened again.

As Ali Baba hurried away, a single coin fell from his bag. But he was in such a hurry that he didn't notice it lying in the sun.

Ali Baba and his wife used the money to open a shop. They hired a clever, loyal girl named Morgiana to help them at home and work in the store with their son. Ali Baba gave everyone a fair price, and the townspeople were happy to shop there.

Meanwhile, when the band of thieves returned to the cave, the captain noticed something shiny on the ground: it was the very coin that Ali Baba had dropped some days before. Realizing that someone had discovered the cave and its treasures, he instructed his men to go into town and find out if anyone had recently become rich.

In the town square, one thief overheard some women talking about Ali Baba's shop.

"Ali Baba has the best merchandise," said the first woman.

"Yes," said the other woman, "but I've always wondered how a woodcutter managed to open his own shop."

The thief couldn't believe it! Was it possible that Ali Baba had visited the secret cave? He might have used the gold to open his shop!

That evening, the thief hid outside the shop and waited until Morgiana left. He sneakily followed her to Ali Baba's house, and then marked the door with chalk and hurried off to tell the captain that he had found Ali Baba.

The thief thought he had been quite clever, but little did he know that Morgiana had seen him! Sure that he was up to no good, she decided to trick him. After he left, she took a piece of chalk and marked all the houses on the street.

Late at night, the thieves rode into town. When they reached Ali Baba's street, they were shocked to see all of the doors marked with chalk. Furious, they went back to the cave to make a new plan.

A few evenings later, the captain disguised himself as a merchant. He went to Ali Baba's store, happy to find Ali Baba there.

"Hello, good sir," he said. "I have some oil to sell at the market tomorrow morning, but I have nowhere to sleep tonight. Do you have room in your home for a humble merchant and his donkeys?"

Ali Baba looked at the line of donkeys with barrels strapped to their backs, and kindly invited the man to spend the night at his house. Little did he know that the barrels did not contain oil—instead, a thief was hiding in each one!

The captain of the thieves followed Ali Baba home, bringing the donkeys into the yard. He bent down beside each barrel and whispered to his men: "When you hear my signal, leap out of the barrels and we'll get our revenge on Ali Baba."

Later that night, after everyone else had gone to bed, Morgiana's lamp ran out of oil. She went into the yard to fetch some from the merchant's barrels, knowing that Ali Baba would pay for whatever she took.

As Morgiana approached the nearest barrel, a voice called out: "Is it time, master?"

Morgiana was shocked, but reacted quickly.

"Not yet, but soon," she answered.

She hurriedly gathered some straw and laid it beside each barrel. She lit the straw on fire with a torch, causing clouds of smoke to fill the barrels. The thieves began coughing and choking. Afraid of being burned, they jumped out of the barrels and ran far away.

Morgiana quietly put out the fire and went back inside. A short time later, she heard the phony merchant calling from his window. When his men did not respond, he went to check the barrels. He was shocked to discover them empty! Furious, he snuck away to hatch another plan.

In the morning, Ali Baba wondered where the merchant had gone. Morgiana showed him the empty barrels and explained all that had happened in the night. She also told him about the chalk mark on the door, sure that it was related. Ali Baba was very thankful for what she had done.

Meanwhile, the captain was outraged that his band of thieves had run off. He was more determined than ever to get revenge on Ali Baba! He hatched a new plan: he would open a shop across from Ali Baba's store, and spend time befriending Ali Baba and his family until he finally had a chance for revenge.

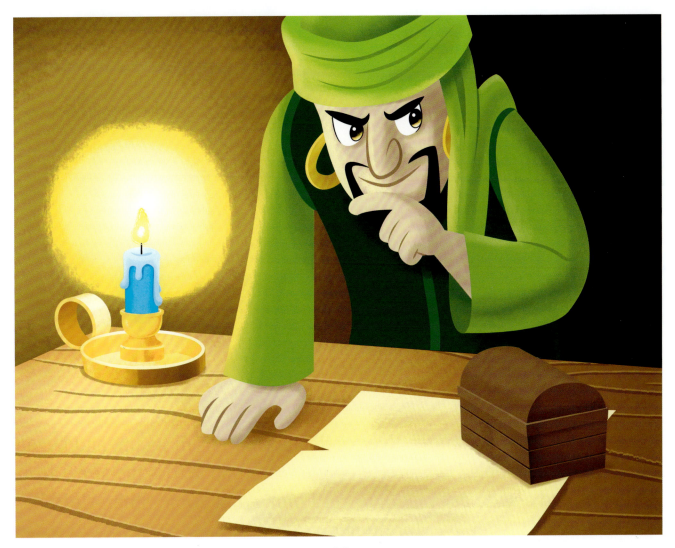

And so the captain of the thieves disguised himself again, and began using the name Cogia Hassan. He opened his shop across the street from Ali Baba, and acted very kindly toward him. After some time, Ali Baba invited Cogia Hassan over for dinner.

While they dined, Morgiana began to feel suspicious of Cogia Hassan. There was something familiar about him, but she couldn't quite put her finger on it. Just then, he leaned over and Morgiana saw a dagger stashed in his robe. She realized that he was the captain of the thieves, and he'd come to hurt Ali Baba!

Morgiana hatched her own plan to stop the scoundrel from hurting Ali Baba and his family. Calling for a servant to play music, she began to dance, waving a long, flowing scarf in front of her. As she danced around the table, Morgiana kept a watchful eye on Cogia Hassan. When she stepped behind him, she quickly wrapped the scarf around him, and tied him up.

"Morgiana!" cried Ali Baba. "What are you doing to our honorable guest?"

"This is no honorable guest! Don't you recognize him? He is the captain of the thieves!" Morgiana replied, revealing the dagger.

At that, Ali Baba and his son seized the dagger and summoned the police, who sent the villain directly to prison.

"Thank you, Morgiana," said Ali Baba. "We owe you our lives. Marry my son and join our family, for I already care for you like a daughter."

From that day on, Ali Baba and his family lived happily ever after. Their children and grandchildren had everything they wanted, for they only had to utter the secret words "Open, sesame" to gain entrance to the hidden cave of riches.